Nighttime:
Too Dark to See

Nighttime:
Too Dark to See

by Todd Strasser

Scholastic Inc.

New York Toronto London Auckland Sydney
Mexico City New Delhi Hong Kong Buenos Aires

For Gina and Matt with thanks.
T. S.

ISBN-13: 978-0-439-80068-6
ISBN-10: 0-439-80068-4

12 11 10 9 8 7 6 5 4 3 2 1   8 9 10 11 12 13/0

Printed in the U.S.A.
First printing, February 2008

CONTENTS

The Thing Under the Bed

"What are you doing?" Justin Porter asked his little sister, Amanda. Justin was eleven years old. He was in the hallway outside Amanda's room. Amanda was seven. She was standing on the chair next to her bed. Amanda was wearing her pink pajama bottoms and a pink T-shirt. She was holding her white unicorn and her tattered old "banky" in her arms. Her "banky" was all that was left of her favorite pink baby blanket.

"I'm getting into bed," said Amanda.

"If you're getting into bed, why are you standing on that chair?" Justin asked.

"Because," said Amanda.

"Because what?" said Justin.

"Go away," said Amanda.

"Because you're going to jump from that chair to your bed," Justin said. "Because you're afraid."

Amanda scrunched her face up like she was going to cry. It was true that she was afraid. Her bed had long legs, and there was a big space under it. She was afraid that if she stood too close to the space, something would reach out and grab her. So every night, she gathered her unicorn and "banky" in her arms and climbed up on the chair beside the bed. Then, holding those things very tightly, she jumped from the chair to the bed.

"There's nothing to be afraid of," Justin said. "There's nothing under your bed."

Amanda didn't move from the chair. As long as her brother was there, she wouldn't jump to the bed. "Go away," she said, trying her best not to cry.

But Justin didn't go away. He went over to the

bed and got down on his hands and knees. "Hey, Thing Under the Bed," he said. "Come out, come out wherever you are."

Amanda held her breath. Her heart raced. She knew the thing under the bed was there. Sometimes, at night, she heard it breathing.

"Come on, Thing Under the Bed," Justin said. "If you're here, show yourself."

A moment later, he backed away from the bed. "See? There's nothing there. If there was, it would have gotten me by now."

"Mom!" Amanda cried.

"Scaredy-cat," Justin snarled, and backed out of the room.

A moment later, Mrs. Porter arrived. "What's wrong, hon?"

"Justin's teasing me!" Amanda said.

Mrs. Porter looked in Justin's room. Amanda's brother was sitting on the floor, pretending to play with his Legos.

"Don't tease your sister, Justin," his mother said.

While her mother's back was turned, Amanda jumped from the chair to the bed. Then she crawled nder the covers and clutched her unicorn and "banky" tight. Mrs. Porter came into the room and tucked her in. She kissed Amanda on the forehead and whispered, "When I was your age, I was afraid, too."

Mrs. Porter left the door open and the hall light on and went into her room. Amanda lay very still and listened. She wasn't sure, but she thought she heard the thing under the bed rustle. But she knew that as long as she was under the covers she was safe. Soon she fell asleep.

The next evening, just before Amanda's bedtime, Justin crawled under her bed. He crawled to the very far corner and curled up so that his sister wouldn't see him. Then he waited.

A little while later, he saw his sister's feet come into the room. He heard the chair squeak as she climbed up on it. He heard the soft *thump!* when she jumped from the chair to the bed. The bedcovers rustled as she snuggled under them.

A few moments later, Mrs. Porter came to tuck in her daughter.

Justin waited until his mother turned off the

bedroom light and left the room. Then he started to breathe loudly. He scraped his fingers against the carpet under the bed like a monster with claws. He made a deep monster groan.

"Mommy!" In the bed above him, Amanda shrieked with fear. *Thump!* Her feet hit the floor, and she ran as fast as she could out of the room.

Justin grinned. All he had to do now was get out from under the bed and back into his room. He'd pretend to be playing with his Legos. He'd pretend he knew nothing about what had happened in his sister's room.

He started to crawl.

His fingers scraped against the carpet under the bed.

But he didn't move.

He couldn't get out from under the bed.

Something was holding him from behind.

The Open Door

Tara Richards was in bed. The small green night-light by the door glowed. The radiator gurgled and hissed. She yawned. Both of her parents had already come in to say good night. Tara's eyes were growing heavy. She rolled over and felt her head sink into the pillow. She was just about to close her eyes when she noticed that the closet door was opened a little bit.

Tara sat up and hugged her teddy. "Mom! Dad!" she called.

"What is it, Tara?" her mother answered from her bedroom.

"My closet's open," Tara called back.

"Just close it, hon," called her father.

"I can't," Tara called back. "I'm scared."

Tara heard her mother whisper and her father mutter. The springs of her parents' bed squeaked. A moment later, her father appeared in her doorway. "Suppose I stand here and watch while you close the closet?" he said.

Tara clutched her teddy and shook her head. "It's scary."

"You can't expect us to come in and close your closet door every time you leave it open," her father said.

Tara knew that her father was annoyed. "It's just at night," she said.

"You can't expect us to come in every night," said her father.

Mrs. Richards joined her husband in the

doorway. "What's wrong? Why haven't you come back to bed?"

"I'm trying to explain to Tara that she can't expect us to come in every night and close her closet door for her," said Mr. Richards.

"Is it really such a big deal?" Mrs. Richards asked her husband.

"No, but it's silly," said Mr. Richards. "There's nothing in her closet. And there's no reason she can't close it herself."

"There *could* be something in there," said Tara.

"You're getting too old for that," said her father.

"I don't think that's fair," Tara's mother said to her husband. "I can't go to sleep unless all the closet doors in our room are closed."

"You're too old for that, too," Mr. Richards told his wife.

"Then why do you make sure all the downstairs doors are locked every night?" Mrs. Richards asked her husband.

"That's different," said Tara's father. "Someone could come in."

"Who?" asked his wife. "We live way out in the country. Our nearest neighbor is half a mile away."

"Doesn't matter," said Mr. Richards.

"And what about the garage door?" asked Mrs. Richards.

"Someone might take something," said her husband.

"If you can't go to bed without being sure all those doors are closed, then you should understand why Tara can't go to bed unless her closet door is closed," said Mrs. Richards. Then she stepped into Tara's room and closed the closet door tightly.

The next morning, Tara woke early. Her room was filled with sunlight. Tara stretched and yawned. She turned her head.

Her closet door was open.

Tara caught her breath and tensed. Suddenly, she felt fully awake. Clutching her teddy, she slid out of bed and quickly inched across the room, never taking her eyes off the open closet door. When she reached the room doorway, she sprinted into her parents' room.

Her parents were still asleep. Tara crawled over

the bed and got under the covers with them. They both woke up.

"What are you doing?" her mother asked with a yawn.

Tara told her about the closet door being open.

Mr. Richards turned to his wife. "I thought you closed it last night."

"I did." Mrs. Richards yawned and stretched. "It must have popped open on its own."

"It never did that before," Tara said.

"Don't worry." Mrs. Richards put her arms around Tara and hugged her.

But then Tara felt her mother's arms stiffen.

"Why is *our* closet open?" Mrs. Richards asked. Tara could hear the alarm in her mother's voice.

Tara and her father sat up in bed. Across the room, the double doors of her parents' closet were wide open.

"I guess you forgot to close them," said Mr. Richards.

"I didn't forget," Tara's mother said firmly. "I closed those doors last night. Just like I do every night."

"Are you *certain?*" Mr. Richards asked.

"Yes," said Mrs. Richards.

"Then I guess the monster in the closet opened them," said Tara's father.

"Mom!" Tara gasped fearfully and hugged her mother.

"That's not funny," Mrs. Richards scolded her husband. Then she stroked Tara's head. "Don't be afraid. There are no monsters in our closets."

"Then why was mine open this morning?" Tara asked. "And why is yours open?"

Mrs. Richards looked at her husband.

"Don't ask me," said Mr. Richards.

"It doesn't bother you?" Mrs. Richards asked her husband.

"Not at all," said Tara's father.

"How do you explain that *both* closets are open?" Tara's mother asked.

"I can't," answered her husband. "But the one thing I do know is that no one snuck into our house last night while we were asleep and opened them."

"How do you know?" asked Tara.

"Because I know I locked all the downstairs doors

last night," said Mr. Richards. "No one could have come in."

"Are you *certain*?" asked his wife.

"Yes," said her husband.

Just then, they all heard a creak from downstairs. Tara's parents shared a look.

"That sounded like a door," said Mrs. Richards.

Mr. Richards frowned and got out of bed. He pulled on his robe and went out into the upstairs hallway. The air in the hallway felt colder than usual. Mr. Richards wondered if the heat had gone off during the night.

He started down the stairs but stopped halfway.

The front door was wide open.

Cold air was blowing in.

Mr. Richards felt a chill.

He was certain he'd locked that door the night before.

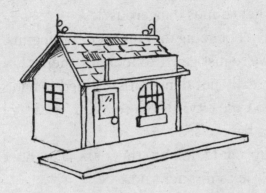

The Silver Ghost

Each summer, Alex Crane and his mom went to visit their cousins in the country. Alex always looked forward to the visit because he got to spend time with his cousin David. Together they would play ball and hunt frogs and climb trees.

"Can Alex and I stay out after dark tonight?" David asked his parents at dinner on the first night Alex and his mom were there. "We want to go owl hunting."

"Oh, no," Mrs. Crane said quickly. "I don't want you wandering around in the woods at night with guns. That sounds dangerous."

"We're not going to hunt them with guns," David said. "We're just going to look for them."

"It's really not dangerous," added David's father. "This isn't the city. Out here in the country nothing bad ever happens."

"They could fall in the dark and hurt themselves," Alex's mother said.

David's father turned to the boys. "You boys promise to take flashlights and stay together, right?"

"We will!" Alex and David said.

As soon as dinner was over, David and Alex each took a flashlight and went out into the dark. Above them, the stars twinkled and the moon glowed. Alex felt nervous. In the city, he was never allowed to go out after dark. In the city, bad things happened all the time.

"Let's go this way," said David. He led Alex across his backyard and through the tall grass beyond that. They came to a steep gravel slope. At the bottom were train tracks. David started to scramble down the slope.

"Are you sure this is safe?" Alex asked. "What if a train comes?"

"Don't worry," David said. "These tracks haven't been used in years."

Alex shined his flashlight at the tracks. They did look old and brown with rust. Tall green weeds grew between the railroad ties. He went down the slope and joined David at the bottom.

He and David walked along the tracks. They aimed their flashlights down at the old wooden railroad ties so that they didn't trip. Soon the tracks entered some dark woods. Tall shadowy trees rose up on both sides of them. Alex felt nervous. The woods looked scary. Alex knew the train tracks were supposed to be abandoned. But what if a train did come and they had to run into those woods? Even with a flashlight, Alex didn't feel safe.

"Listen real carefully," David whispered. "This is where the owls are."

Alex listened. He heard the rustle of the leaves

in the trees. Then, from the distance came a faint sound that scared him. "It's a train!" He gasped.

"No, silly, that's an owl," said David.

"But it sounded like the toot of a train whistle," said Alex.

"Not a toot," said David. "A hoot. You'd know it if you'd heard an owl before."

It was true that Alex had never heard an owl hoot before.

David aimed his flashlight toward the dark trees beside the railroad tracks. "Let's go," he said.

"Into the woods?" Alex swallowed nervously.

"You want to see the owl, don't you?" David asked.

Alex wasn't sure he wanted to see the owl enough to go into those woods. David seemed to understand. "Okay, you wait here. I'll go look for the owl. If I find it, I'll come back and get you."

"But your father said we should stay together," Alex said.

"I've been in the woods alone lots of times," David said. "It's no big deal. Just wait here. If I find that owl, I'll come right back and get you."

Before Alex could argue, David disappeared into the dark woods.

Alex stood on the tracks and waited. He looked up at the twinkling stars and the round glowing moon. He looked at the dark woods. He waited. And waited. He wondered what he would do if David didn't come back. He wondered what he would do if a train came.

Then he heard that sound again. This time, it was a little bit louder and sounded a little bit closer. David may have said that it was an owl, but it still sounded like a train to Alex. He looked down the tracks in one direction, and then the other. About a hundred yards away was a small, dark building. Alex was surprised that he hadn't noticed it before. Suddenly, through a window, a faint dot of yellow light glowed as if someone was lighting something.

Alex walked closer. Through the window, he thought he saw a small reddish glow inside. He walked closer. Now he could smell the sweet scent of burning pipe tobacco.

Alex walked closer. Now he could see the outline

of someone sitting in the building. It was an old man with a train engineer's cap. He was smoking a pipe. Each time he puffed, the pipe glowed red.

Alex stepped closer. Suddenly, the man turned and looked at him through the window. Frightened, Alex jumped back. Through the window, he saw the man rise. Alex backed away farther. The man with the pipe stepped out onto the porch next to the tracks. Alex felt his stomach begin to knot from nervousness.

The old man took the pipe from his mouth and said, "Howdy."

"Uh, hi," Alex said.

"Nice night, huh?" said the man.

Alex swallowed. "I guess."

Suddenly, he heard the train whistle sound in the distance. Alex twisted around to look. This time, he was sure it was a train whistle and not an owl. The man reached into his pocket and took out a watch. "The Silver Ghost, right on time."

"A train?" Alex said.

The old man smiled. "Can't be nothin' else. I'd get off those tracks if I was you."

Alex jumped away from the tracks. He stood in a small clearing between the tracks and the dark woods. The train's whistle sounded again, and now Alex could see a glowing yellow light in the distance.

As he watched, the light grew brighter. Soon Alex could hear the chugging of the train's engine and feel the vibrations through the ground under his feet.

Toot! Tooooooooooot! The train's whistle blew. With a loud rumble, it roared past. Alex felt the wind in his face. The branches above him swayed and the leaves rustled. He could smell the oil and diesel fuel. The ground under his feet trembled. He stepped back even farther.

The train passed. The leaves continued to rustle, and the weeds and tall grass beside the tracks swayed. The wind quickly eased, and the roar grew dim.

Down the tracks, Alex saw a flashlight beam come out of the woods. It was David. Alex ran toward him. "Did you see it?"

David shook his head. "I looked all over. I heard it, but I couldn't see it."

"Not the owl," Alex said. "The train."

David made a face. "What train?"

"The Silver Ghost. It just came by — just before you came out of the woods. You had to have seen it. And even if you didn't, you would have heard it."

"I didn't hear anything," David said. "I told you these tracks are abandoned."

"No, they're not," Alex insisted. "The Silver Ghost just came by. I mean, it must have been going a hundred miles per hour!"

David shook his head. "Why do you think it was called the Silver Ghost?"

"Because the old man said so," Alex said.

"What old man?"

"The one with the pipe." Alex turned and pointed at the dark building.

But there was no building there.

And no old man.

Alex took a deep sniff. The smell of pipe tobacco was still in the air. He was about to ask David if he smelled it. But then he changed his mind. No matter what he said, David would never believe him.

What's Behind You?

It was Mother's Day, and Mr. Hill surprised his wife with a big arrangement of flowers. In the kitchen, young Katie Hill helped her mother put the flowers in a glass vase. There were so many flowers that the vase had to be perfectly balanced or it would fall over.

"Maybe we should divide the flowers into two vases," Mrs. Hill said. "Then it won't tip so easily."

"But they look so nice when they're all together," Katie said.

"I guess you're right," said her mother. "We'll just be careful."

When they were finished, they put the vase of flowers in the middle of the kitchen table.

Later that night, Mr. Hill tucked Katie into bed.

"Good night, Daddy," Katie said. "Those flowers were really pretty. Mom loves them."

"I'm glad," her father said. "Now good night, Katie. Sleep tight. Don't let the bedbugs bite."

"I won't, Daddy," Katie said with a yawn.

Mr. Hill went to the door and turned out the bedroom light. "See you in the morning."

Katie closed her eyes and went to sleep. She was the youngest in her family, and each evening she went to bed first. The rest of her family would go to sleep later. They all thought that Katie — like most little girls — stayed in bed and slept all night.

But Katie Hill had a secret. Almost every night, she got out of bed and went downstairs to the kitchen for a snack. It was always very late, long after the rest of her family had gone to sleep. The house was always dark and quiet. Katie was always scared. But as long as she had Midnight with her, she felt safe.

Midnight was the Hills' Labrador retriever. He was jet-black from the tip of his nose to the tip of his tail. Even his nails were black. In the dark, he was almost invisible. Every night, Midnight slept on the floor beside Katie's bed. He did not come into her room until everyone else had gone to sleep.

And every night when Katie went downstairs for her snack, Midnight followed her.

That night, after she fell asleep, Katie had a bad dream. She dreamed that her older brother, Tom, and Midnight were roughhousing in the kitchen. There was a crash when Tom accidentally knocked over the vase of Mother's Day flowers. The vase crashed to the floor and shattered, sending sharp shards of glass everywhere. Midnight stepped on a shard and howled in pain. The broken glass went deep into his paw.

Katie woke. She was breathing hard and felt frightened. She loved Midnight very much and didn't want anything bad to happen to him. She lay in the dark and listened. The house was quiet and still. She could hear the dog breathing on the floor beside her bed. Katie reached over the side of her bed. She touched the dog's fur and felt his ribs rise and fall as he slept.

Katie felt a wave of relief. It was only a dream. Everything was okay. She went back to sleep.

A little while later, Katie woke again. Now she was hungry. It was time for her nightly visit to the kitchen.

She slipped out of bed and walked quietly across the room. Behind her the dog rose and followed. Katie went down the stairs. The steady breaths behind her made her feel safe. She always wanted Midnight to stay behind her. She could rely on her own eyes to see what was ahead of her, but not what was behind. That was Midnight's job.

Downstairs, they walked through the shadows toward the kitchen. When they crossed the dining room, Katie heard the click of dog nails on the floor behind her.

They entered the kitchen. Something seemed different, but in the dark Katie wasn't sure what it was. And she never turned on the lights, for fear of waking her family.

Katie opened the pantry. Just as she did every night, she took out three chocolate chip cookies. While she stood at the counter eating a cookie with her right hand, she took another cookie in her left hand and held it down for Midnight. Katie felt the dog take the cookie out of her hand. She felt the hardness of his teeth and the wetness of his tongue on her fingers.

Katie ate her second cookie and left the kitchen. Once again, she heard the click of nails on the floor as she went through the dining room. She heard the dog pant lightly as they climbed back up the stairs. In her room, she got back into bed. She reached down and patted the dog gently, then went to sleep.

In the morning when Katie woke up, Midnight wasn't on the floor beside her bed. Katie wasn't surprised. The dog often rose early and went downstairs to be let out. Katie got out of bed and went down. In the kitchen, Mr. and Mrs. Hill were sitting quietly at the table. Now Katie realized what had been different when she entered the kitchen the night before.

"Where are the flowers?" she asked.

"Tom and Midnight were running around last night, and they accidentally knocked over the vase," Mrs. Hill said.

Katie looked around. "Where's Tom, anyway? And where's Midnight?"

"Tom's still sleeping," Mr. Hill said. "And Midnight is at the twenty-four-hour emergency vet. When the vase broke, he cut his paw very badly."

Katie was confused. "This morning?"

"No, last night," said Mrs. Hill. "Just after you went to sleep. The vet wanted to keep Midnight overnight to make sure he'd be okay."

"But Midnight was here last night," said Katie.

"No, honey, he was at the vet," said Mrs. Hill.

"That can't be," said Katie.

"Why not?" asked Mr. Hill.

Katie didn't answer. She felt a shiver and stared down at her hand. If Midnight hadn't eaten out of it last night, then what had?

Game Boy

Peter Lenox played so many videogames that his friends called him Game Boy. Peter played his PSP at the kitchen table when he ate breakfast. Then he played it while he walked to the bus stop. He played it while he waited for the bus, and he played it while he rode on the bus.

Everyone knew that you got in trouble if you were caught by a teacher playing videogames at school. But sometimes Peter couldn't resist. At least once a week, a teacher would catch Peter playing his PSP and take it away. Peter would have to wait until after school to get it back. That meant missing the bus home. But Peter didn't care. He just walked home playing the PSP.

Each day when Peter got home, he stopped playing videogames just long enough to do his homework and his chores. He stopped just long enough to eat dinner and practice violin for twenty minutes. He stopped and read ten pages in a book. But he spent every other waking second playing.

Peter's parents didn't know what to do. Peter got good grades in school. He was a well-behaved and obedient boy. If Mrs. Lenox asked him to help with the dishes after dinner, he would always help. And then he would go play videogames. If Mr. Lenox asked him to take out the garbage, Peter would do it right away, and then play videogames.

Mr. and Mrs. Lenox got tired of trying to think of ways to keep their son from playing videogames every second of the day. Sometimes it was easier to let him play. But it still bothered them very much.

"Isn't there anything else you want to do?" Mrs. Lenox asked.

Peter shook his head. He stared at the screen of his PSP. His thumbs moved so fast they were a blur.

"Is there anything we can do to get you to turn that thing off?" Mr. Lenox asked.

"Why?" Peter asked, without looking up.

"Because playing videogames all the time can't be good for you," said his father.

"Why not?" asked Peter.

"Because it can't be," Mr. Lenox said.

"But I get good grades in school and practice violin every night and do all the chores you ask me to do," Peter said.

"You could spend more time outside," said Mrs. Lenox.

"I have allergies," said Peter.

This was true. Whenever Peter went outside, his eyes began to itch and swell. His nose began to run, and he would sneeze and cough.

"You could spend more time with your friends," said Mr. Lenox.

"They're always busy," Peter said.

This was also true. Peter's friends played sports. They took lessons and went to tutors. They participated in after school activities. They did homework and practiced their instruments. Some of Peter's friends even avoided him because all he wanted to do was play videogames.

Peter's parents pursed their lips in frustration.

"What's wrong with playing videogames?" Peter asked.

"There's nothing wrong with it as long as it's not the only thing you do," said his father.

"We're just worried that if you play so much you might someday *become* a videogame," said his mother.

Peter gave her a puzzled look.

"Well, not really," Mrs. Lenox said. "But you know what I mean."

The truth was that Peter didn't know what she meant. But it didn't matter. He liked playing videogames, and they didn't hurt anyone.

So Peter played more and more. He didn't notice when his friends spent less time with him. He didn't realize that he didn't talk to people as much as he used to. He wasn't aware that even when he wasn't playing videogames, the game music still played in his head.

Sometimes he even pretended to be the characters in the games.

Sometimes he didn't even need his PSP. He could play a game in his head without it.

At night after the lights went out, he played his PSP under the covers.

His dreams were videogame dreams.

Peter dreamed he was in a videogame. He was playing against the other characters. The videogame music was all around him.

"Peter?" It was his father's voice.

Peter stopped playing and looked around. Through a small video screen, he could see his bedroom. The room was filled with sunlight. The clock beside his bed said 8:37. Peter knew it had to be morning.

"Peter?" On the screen, Peter saw his father step into the bedroom and look around with a puzzled expression.

"Is he there?" Peter heard his mother ask.

On the screen, Peter saw his father shake his head and answer, "No."

Now his mother entered the bedroom. "That's strange," she said with a frown. "Where could he be?"

"Did you check the bathroom?" Peter's father asked.

"Yes," said his mother. "He's not there."

Through the video screen, Peter watched as his father came closer. "He couldn't have gone far because he left his game."

Peter's mother came closer. "It's on," she said.

Peter's parents came closer and closer. Their faces grew larger and larger until they filled the whole screen.

"He wouldn't leave without his game," said his mother.

"That's for sure," said his father.

As Peter watched, two giant hands reached toward the screen. They were Mr. Lenox's hands. The fingers closed around the side of the screen.

Suddenly, the screen bounced and jerked as Mr. Lenox lifted it.

Once again, Peter stared at his parents' faces.

"I can't imagine where he could have gone," said his mother.

"Well, we might as well turn this off," said his father.

No! Peter thought. *Don't!*

But it was too late. Everything went black.

Dead End

Everyone knew that Randall Glass was different. After he was born, his parents moved to the house across from Dead End Road. The big yellow sign at the beginning of the road said DEAD END. When Randall was just a baby and his mother pushed his stroller past that sign, he would always cry.

Later, if a ball rolled onto Dead End Road, he refused to get it. If his friends wanted to ride their bikes down the road, he refused to go.

But Randall was strange in other ways, too. He hated rooms with open windows. He refused to wear anything black. And instead of making a left turn, he would always make three rights. And he would never, ever go down Dead End Road.

When other kids asked why, Randall said, "Do you know what dead end means? It's where the dead end up."

"No, it doesn't," said the other kids. "It means a street that ends and doesn't go anywhere."

Randall shook his head as if they were wrong.

The other kids laughed and teased Randall. But it didn't matter.

David Walsh was Randall's only friend. David was as normal as Randall was strange. When people asked David why he was Randall's friend, he said that Randall was the best friend a kid could have.

When Randall was eight, he and his family moved away. When kids asked David where Randall and his family had gone, David said he didn't know.

"Let's go down here," Tyler Ross said one gray spring day when he and David were riding their bikes. They'd stopped at the entrance to Dead End

Road. Tyler was one of David's many friends. But none of them could replace Randall.

David shook his head.

"Why not?" asked Tyler.

The answer was that Randall had told him never to go down Dead End Road. But David didn't say that. He just shook his head.

"Scared?" Tyler said in a taunting way.

David didn't like kids who teased and taunted. That's why Tyler Ross would never be the kind of friend Randall had been.

"The only things I'm afraid of," David said, "are the things I *should* be afraid of."

"There's nothing scary about a dead end," said Tyler.

"Then go down there yourself," said David.

Tyler looked down Dead End Road. There were no houses on it. Just big old trees with long, bare, gnarled branches. The road was old and full of deep, muddy potholes.

"That road looks really bad," said Tyler. "I'll go down it another time."

The boys started to ride away. Coming toward

them was a dump truck towing a big yellow back-hoe. When the driver saw the boys, he slowed down and waved. David and Tyler stopped.

"You kids know where Dead End Road is?" the driver asked.

David pointed. "Down there. On the left."

"Why are you going there?" asked Tyler.

"We're gonna start digging foundations next week," the driver said.

"For houses?" Tyler guessed.

The driver nodded. "They're building a new housing development back there."

That Friday, David was eating lunch in the school cafeteria when a boy named Billy Leeds came up to him. Billy was a bully and a braggart. David didn't like him. With Billy was Tyler and a boy named Cameron.

"Tyler says you're scared to go down Dead End Road," Billy said.

David chewed his sandwich and didn't answer.

"We're going down there tonight," said Billy. "You want to come with us? Or are you afraid?"

"I'm only afraid of the things I *should* be afraid of," David answered.

"So you won't go?" Billy said.

David shook his head.

"You're chicken," said Billy.

"If you say so," said David.

It was warm that evening. As dark approached, David was outside, shooting baskets in his driveway. David loved basketball. His father had installed outdoor lights so that he could play in the dark. While he was outside, Billy, Tyler, and Cameron rode up.

"Still too scared to come with us?" Billy asked.

David didn't answer. He took another shot with the basketball.

"Chicken," Billy said. Then he and the others rode away, down Dead End Road.

David shot baskets for a little while longer. Then he sat down on the ball and waited in his driveway. He wondered why Randall had told him never to go down Dead End Road. He wondered why he'd never thought to ask.

After a while, he heard the scratchy sounds of tires and heavy breathing and grunts. A few moments later, Billy and Cameron raced past on their bikes so fast that they didn't notice David sitting on the basketball in his driveway. Their eyes were wide with fright.

A second later, David saw Tyler ride out of Dead End Road as fast as he could. Like the other boys, his eyes were wide with fear. David rose to his feet and waved, "Tyler!"

Tyler skidded to a stop on his bike. With wide eyes, he looked at David. Then he looked back at Dead End Road and bit his lip nervously. David walked toward him. Tyler was breathing hard and shaking.

"What happened?" David asked.

"We went down to the end," Tyler said. He was still panting. "The only thing down there was that big yellow backhoe and a field of tall weeds. I didn't like it. There was something creepy about that field. Billy got off his bike and said he wanted to walk into the field to see what was there. Cameron and I didn't want to, but Billy said we were chicken, so we did."

David nodded slowly. Not many boys could let themselves be called a chicken.

"So we walked out into the field," Tyler said. "It wasn't easy because the weeds were really thick and they came up past our knees. Our feet kept getting tangled and caught in them. It felt really creepy. Almost like hands reaching up and trying to grab our ankles. And the deeper into the field we went, the worse it was."

"Billy looked really scared just now when he rode past," David said.

"He was ahead of Cameron and me," Tyler said. "I don't know what happened, but the next thing I knew he let out a yell and started to run back to the bikes. Then Cameron and I were running, too. And every step felt like something was grabbing at our ankles. It was the scariest thing I ever felt. I was really happy to get out of there. And I don't blame you for not wanting to go."

Tyler looked back at the entrance to Dead End

Road. "I'll never go down there again. Right now I just want to go home and get into bed and stay there. See you, David."

David watched Tyler ride away. Then he went into his house.

The next day was Saturday. David was outside shooting baskets again when two police cars came down the street and turned onto Dead End Road. A little while later, more cars came. One car said COUNTY CORONER on its side.

Later, the truck turned off of Dead End Road towing the big yellow backhoe. David waved at the driver to stop.

"I thought you were going to dig foundations for that new development," David said.

"We started, but you won't believe what we found," the driver said. "That field is full of bones. It must be some kind of ancient burial ground. Strangest thing I ever saw. No sign saying it's a cemetery. No tombstones. A whole field of skeletons so close to the surface they could practically reach up and grab you. Not one of them was buried more than six inches deep. The police are down there, trying to figure out where they all came from."

The driver drove away, taking the big yellow backhoe with him. David glanced across the street at the sign that said DEAD END.

Randall was right, he thought. *It's where the dead end up.*

A Safe Place to Stay

Rain splashed against the car's windshield. Even with the windshield wipers swishing back and forth, it was almost impossible to see in the dark.

"We're lost," Mrs. Burke said to her husband.

"The sign on the highway said there was a gas station down this road," said Mr. Burke.

"We've gone at least ten miles," said Mrs. Burke. "I haven't seen a gas station."

"It has to be around here somewhere," said Mr. Burke.

"Why don't we just go back to the highway?" asked Ethan Burke. Ethan was twelve. His little sister, Sara, was eight. They were sitting in the backseat.

Mr. Burke stared at the gas gauge. The red warning light glowed. The needle had dipped below EMPTY. "I'm not sure we have enough gas to get back to the highway," he said. "And even if we did, we definitely don't have enough to make it to the next exit."

Crack! A bolt of lightning lit the sky.

"I'm scared!" Sara wailed in the backseat.

Boom! The crash of thunder from above made them all jump.

"Mommy!" Sara cried. Mrs. Burke reached over the seat and held her daughter's hand.

But there was good news. "I think I saw the gas station when the lightning struck," Mr. Burke said. "It's up ahead."

They drove a little farther in the pouring rain.

"There it is!" Ethan cried, pointing through the

windshield. While he didn't want to admit that he was afraid, he was very happy that he'd seen the station.

A moment later, the Burkes drove up to the gas station. But it was dark. The lights were off.

"It's closed," Mrs. Burke said.

"What'll we do?" asked Ethan.

"I don't know," his father answered, and looked at Mrs. Burke.

"We can't go back to the highway," said Mrs. Burke. "So I guess we'll have to find a place to stay for the night around here."

Mr. Burke peered out into the dark. All he could see was rain. "Where?" he asked.

"We'll have to look for a place," said his wife.

"I don't know if that's a good idea," Mr. Burke said. "What if we start driving and run out of gas before we find a place to stay? We'll be in the middle of nowhere. If we stay here, at least we'll be able to get gas when the station opens in the morning."

"You want to stay in the car all night?" Mrs. Burke asked.

"I don't want to do that!" Sara cried.

"I don't know what other choice we have," said Mr. Burke.

"I promised my sister we'd be at their house by ten in the morning," said Mrs. Burke.

"Let me check something," said Mr. Burke. He took a flashlight out of the glove compartment and then got out of the car. The rest of his family watched while he went up to the gas station door. He shined the flashlight around and then came back and got into the car.

"They open at six in the morning," Mr. Burke said. "If we fill up right at six, we should be able to get to your sister's house by ten."

"I don't want to stay in the car all night!" Sara wailed.

"I don't know what else we can do," said Mr. Burke.

The family sat in the car. The rain crashed down. All around them thunder boomed and lightning flashed and crackled.

"I'm scared!" Sara cried again.

"Come up here," Mrs. Burke said.

Sara climbed into the front seat and curled up in

her mother's lap. Mrs. Burke looked at her husband. "We can't stay like this all night."

Mr. Burke made a decision. He turned up the collar of his raincoat and reached for the flashlight again.

"Where are you going?" his wife asked.

"I'm going to walk down the road," said Mr. Burke.

"In the rain and dark?" Mrs. Burke said.

"I don't know how else to find a place where we can stay," her husband said, and started to open the door.

"Be careful!" Mrs. Burke said.

Mr. Burke got out of the car and turned on the flashlight. His family watched him disappear into the dark and rain.

"What if something happens to him?" Ethan asked nervously.

"Nothing bad is going to happen," Mrs. Burke assured him.

Mrs. Burke and her children waited in the car. The rain hammered down on the roof. Thunder crashed and lightning flashed outside. Ethan's stomach was in knots as he waited for his father to return.

"Why hasn't Daddy come back?" Sara asked after a while.

"I'm sure he's still looking," said Mrs. Burke.

The family waited and waited.

"Seems like he's been gone a long time," Ethan said nervously.

"I'm sure he's okay," replied Mrs. Burke. But inside she was worried, too.

More time passed. By now Sara had fallen asleep in Mrs. Burke's lap. Sara was a big girl for her age, and Mrs. Burke was very uncomfortable. She knew she couldn't spend the night like that.

"Mom, I'm scared," Ethan whispered, hoping he didn't wake up Sara. "Dad should have come back by now."

"Everything will be okay," Mrs. Burke said. But now she was scared, too.

They waited. The rain beat down. Ethan's eyelids grew heavy. But he didn't want to fall asleep.

"Ah!" Suddenly, Mrs. Burke gasped.

Ethan opened his eyes. A stranger was coming out of the dark!

Ethan tensed. He gripped the seat.

Outside, the stranger in the dark reached for the door.

"Mom, do something!" Ethan gasped.

The car door opened. Ethan's heart was pounding. The pouring rain roared.

The stranger stuck his head in through the open door.

It was Mr. Burke.

Ethan and his mother both sighed loudly with relief.

"You scared the daylights out of us," Mrs. Burke said.

"Sorry." Rainwater dripped off Mr. Burke's head and shoulders. "I've got good news." He held up a diamond-shaped piece of green plastic. A key was attached to it.

"You found a place to stay?" Mrs. Burke gasped with delight.

"Sure did," said Mr. Burke as he got into the car.

"It's just up the road." He handed Ethan the key. "Hold this."

"I thought hotels give you a key card," said Ethan.

"This is what they used to give you," said his father as he started to drive. "Back in the day."

Mr. Burke drove around the bend and up a muddy driveway. The car splashed through potholes as they went up a hill. Sara woke up. "What's happening?" she asked with a yawn.

"We're going to a place where we can sleep," said her mother.

The car bounced up the old driveway. The windshield wipers swished back and forth. Soon a row of small old brown cabins came into view.

"What is this?" Ethan asked.

"These are bungalows," explained his father. "This is the way motels were set up in the old days."

"The *real* old days," said Mrs. Burke.

Mr. Burke parked the car beside one of the bungalows. He opened the door and the family hurried through the rain and inside. The walls of the bungalow were made of yellow wood. The refrigerator was small and rounded. The kitchen table and chairs had metal legs.

"What's that funny smell?" Ethan asked.

"Propane," said Mr. Burke. "It's for the heater and the stove. No one uses it anymore."

"Why not?" Ethan asked.

"Too dangerous," said Mr. Burke. "Every now and then, a propane tank would explode."

"We're not in danger, are we?" asked Mrs. Burke.

"Not if we're staying here just one night," said Mr. Burke. "I mean, think of how old this place is. If it hasn't burned up yet, I'm sure it will last one more night."

"That's not funny," said Mrs. Burke.

"This place is way old," said Ethan.

"It's also way warm and dry and a lot more comfortable than spending the night in the car," said Mr. Burke. He checked his watch. "Enough talking. We better get to bed. We have to get up early and hit the road."

Sara slept on the couch. Ethan's parents took one bedroom and gave Ethan the other. Ethan slid into the bed. The sheets were rough and the blanket was scratchy. The pillow was hard and smelled like soap. But Ethan was tired and went right to sleep.

The next thing Ethan knew, his father was shaking his shoulder. Sunlight came in through the window. "Time to get up," Mr. Burke said. "We need to get going or we'll be late."

Still half asleep, Sara and Ethan climbed into the backseat of the car. It had stopped raining, and the sun had just risen over the distant hills. But the dirt driveway was still muddy.

"Don't you have to pay?" Mrs. Burke asked her husband.

"I paid last night," Mr. Burke said. "The owner told me to leave the key in the room when we left this morning."

Mr. Burke drove down the driveway and out onto the road. They went around the bend to the gas station. Even though the sun was out, rainwater still dripped off the gas station roof. Mr. Burke parked the car next to a gas pump. He checked his watch. "We're a few minutes early," he said.

The family waited in the car. Outside the sun continued to rise. At a few minutes after six A.M. an old red pickup truck pulled into the gas station. A large man with a gray beard and a red shirt got out. He frowned when he saw the Burkes' car.

Mr. Burke rolled down the car window. "Boy, are we glad to see you," he said.

"You haven't been here all night, have you?" the man asked.

"We got here last night, but you were closed," said Mr. Burke. "So we stayed in one of those bungalows around the bend."

The man's bushy gray eyebrows rose. "You did, did you?"

"Yes, sir," said Mr. Burke. "We all got a good night's sleep. And as soon as you fill up the tank, we'll be on our way."

The man started to fill the car's tank with gas. "Said you stayed in one of those bungalows, did you?" he said.

"Yes, sir," said Mr. Burke.

"The ones right around the corner?"

"That's correct," said Mr. Burke.

"Interesting," the man said, and finished pumping the gas.

Mr. Burke paid him. "Strange fellow," he said as they drove away from the gas station.

"Why do you say that, Dad?" Ethan asked.

"He acted like he didn't believe we stayed at those bungalows," said Mr. Burke.

"I wonder why," said Mrs. Burke.

They drove around the bend on their way back to the highway. As they passed the driveway to the bungalows, Ethan noticed something strange. "Dad, stop."

Mr. Burke stopped. A rusty, old metal gate crossed the driveway. It was held closed by a rusty chain. Up on the hill, all that remained of the bungalows were a few charred chimneys. Between them were the blackened stumps of trees.

Hanging on the locked gate was a sign that said CLOSED DUE TO FIRE.

Dance Lessons

"It's time for you to take dancing lessons," Mrs. Phelps said one night at dinner.

Stephen Phelps shook his head. "No way."

"It's what young men do when they enter the fifth grade," said his mother.

"Not me," said Stephen.

Mrs. Phelps glanced at her husband for help.

"I went when I was your age," his father said.

"And all your friends are going," added Mrs. Phelps.

The next day at school, Stephen asked his best friend, Gary Wells, if he was going to go.

"It's not a big deal," Gary said. "Everybody does it. You go for two hours on Friday nights, and then someone's mother or father takes us out for ice cream."

"What if you ask a girl to dance and she says no?" Stephen asked.

"It's not allowed," said Gary. "If you ask, they have to say yes."

Stephen wasn't convinced, but he decided to give it a try. That Friday night he put on a white shirt and a tie and his blue blazer.

"Have fun," Mr. Phelps said when he dropped Stephen off at the recreation center. Stephen doubted he'd have fun. When he saw the girls in their dresses and white gloves and black patent-leather shoes, he thought they looked silly. He felt a little better when he saw Gary arrive.

"What do we do?" Stephen asked nervously as they went inside.

"Just do whatever they tell you to do," Gary whispered.

An old lady named Miss Maples taught the lessons. A group of boys and girls from the high school acted as her assistants. The high school boys helped teach the fifth-grade girls, and the high school girls helped the fifth-grade boys.

Stephen did what he was told. They showed him how to ask a girl to dance and how to offer his hand.

But the best part of the dance lesson came later when Gary's mother took them all out for ice cream.

Each week, Stephen learned a little more about dancing, but he didn't like it. When it was time to practice, he wouldn't dance with a girl his own age. He would only dance with one of the older dance instructors. The best part of each lesson was always going out for ice cream with his friends.

No one told Stephen that the last lesson of the year was a real dance. That night, Stephen and Gary and the other boys stood on one side of the dance floor, and the girls stood on the other. The boys whispered and the girls giggled. The music started, and Miss Maples told the boys to cross the dance floor and ask a girl to dance. Stephen looked around. The high school boys and girls were sitting in chairs against the far wall. Tonight they weren't there to dance.

"You can't ask a high school girl to dance with you this time," Gary whispered in Stephen's ear. "You have to ask a girl our age."

Stephen felt a chill. So far he'd managed to avoid dancing with a girl his own age. All around him, boys bit their lips and stared at their feet. Across the floor, the girls stood in groups, whispering and giggling.

"Don't wait too long," Gary whispered. "The best dancers always get picked first."

One by one, the boys on Stephen's side of the room crossed the dance floor. Stephen froze. His forehead felt hot and his palms were moist. His feet wouldn't move.

"Time to go," Gary said, and started across the floor.

Stephen watched his friend walk up to a tall girl

with curly hair. Her name was Elise and she was a good dancer.

More and more boys were asking girls to dance. The floor began to fill with dancing couples. Gary was dancing with Elise, but he kept looking over at Stephen. Stephen knew his friend wanted him to pick a partner and dance. He knew that soon he would be the only one left.

But Stephen felt paralyzed. He knew that asking a girl to dance should not have been a big deal. It would be much worse to be the only boy left without a dance partner. If he danced, no one would care. But if he didn't dance, kids would talk about it at school tomorrow.

And yet, he couldn't get himself to ask.

Suddenly, a girl with long brown hair stepped through the doorway. She was wearing a yellow dress and white gloves and black shoes. Stephen had never seen her before. He didn't know who she was, but he knew she was the one he would dance with.

Stephen quickly crossed the floor. He was afraid some other boy might get there first. But no one did. He remembered how to introduce himself. The girl said her name was Dawn. Stephen asked her to dance and offered his hand. Her hand felt as light as a feather.

Stephen led her to the dance floor and held her the way he'd been taught. Soon they were moving together to the music. Dawn moved as lightly as an angel. As far as Stephen was concerned, she was the best dancer — and the prettiest girl — in the whole dance.

Together, Stephen and Dawn danced around the floor. Dawn followed his lead perfectly. Not once did she step on his foot, or did he step on hers. As they danced, other couples moved out of their way. Some kids smiled. Others frowned. Stephen knew that the ones who frowned were jealous because his partner was the best and prettiest dancer.

Stephen was sorry when the song ended. He didn't want the music to stop. He wanted to keep dancing with Dawn all night long. But it was now time for the boys to get their partners some refreshments. Stephen walked Dawn to the girls' side of the room and told her to wait while he got punch for both of them. Then he hurried to join the other boys around the punch bowl.

The other boys grinned and winked at him. Stephen smiled to himself. He knew they all wished they'd waited until Dawn arrived. Then Gary joined him by the punch bowl.

"What are you doing?" Gary hissed at his friend.

"I'm getting my partner some punch," Stephen said.

"What partner?" Gary whispered.

"Dawn," Stephen said. "The girl I was dancing with."

"You were dancing alone," Gary said.

"What are you talking about?" Stephen said. "Everyone saw me dancing with her."

"Everyone saw you dancing by yourself," Gary said. "Everyone thinks you're crazy."

"You're the one who's crazy," Stephen said. "Or should I say, jealous?"

Stephen picked up two cups of punch and headed back to the girls' side of the room. The girls smiled when he passed them. Some leaned toward their friends and whispered.

Stephen went back to the spot where he'd left Dawn, but she wasn't there. He looked around the room. He asked the girls if anyone had seen the pretty brown-haired girl in the yellow dress. No one had. He asked if they knew a girl named Dawn. No one did. He asked the high school kids and Miss Maples. No one had seen her. He went out into the hall, but it was empty. Then he went outside into the dark.

The sky was a checkerboard pattern of clouds and darkness. Stephen looked around, but all he saw were trees and parked cars.

"Dawn!" he yelled. "Dawn?"

There was no answer.

Stephen walked all the way around the center, calling Dawn's name.

No one answered.

By now, he knew she was gone.

He looked back at the building. The lights were on and he could hear music. The next song had begun. Everyone was dancing again. He knew if he went back, the kids would smile at him. Some would snicker. They would all think he was crazy.

Even worse, he would have to ask a different girl to dance.

Stephen knew he wasn't crazy. And the only girl he wanted to dance with was Dawn. She was real. He knew what she felt like and what she smelled like.

Stephen started to walk away from the center. "Dawn!" he called. "Dawn?"

He knew she was out there somewhere.

He just had to find her.